Three Toy Stories

Adapted by
Kristen L. Depken

Random House New York

 Published in the United States by Random House Children's Books, a division of
Random House, Inc., 1745 Broadway, New York, NY 10019, and in Canada by Random House of Canada Limited, Toronto,
in conjunction with Disney Enterprises, Inc. Random House and the colophon are registered trademarks of Random House, Inc.

ISBN: 978-0-7364-2811-8

www.randomhouse.com/kids

MANUFACTURED IN SINGAPORE

10 9 8 7 6 5 4 3 2

Disney · PIXAR
TOY
STORY

Andy had many toys. But his favorite was a cowboy named Sheriff Woody. Andy and Woody had many fun adventures together.

Andy didn't know it, but when he wasn't around, Woody walked, talked, and had his own adventures. In fact, all of Andy's toys did!

One day, Woody called the toys together for a meeting. He reminded them that Andy and his family would be moving to a new home in just one week.

Then Woody made an important announcement: "Andy's birthday party has been moved to today."

The toys were worried. Birthdays meant new toys, and no one wanted to be replaced.

On the day of Andy's party, the toys watched anxiously as a brand-new toy arrived in Andy's room. The toy had fancy buttons and gadgets. He even had wings!

"I am Buzz Lightyear," the new toy said. Buzz was a space ranger toy—but he thought he was a *real* space ranger.

Woody was not impressed.

LIGHTYEAR

But the other toys loved Buzz—and so did Andy. Andy took down his cowboy posters and hung up space ranger posters. His cowboy bedspread was replaced by a space ranger bedspread. Had Buzz become Andy's new favorite toy?

Woody felt very sad.

One evening, Andy was going to Pizza Planet with his family, and he was only allowed to bring one toy. Woody tried to push Buzz behind a desk so that Andy wouldn't be able to find him. But Buzz fell out the window!

"It was an accident!" Woody told the other toys. They didn't believe him.

Woody got to go to Pizza Planet with Andy. Buzz managed to climb into the car, too. But on the way, Buzz and Woody began to fight, and soon both toys fell out of the car.

"You are delaying my rendezvous with Star Command," Buzz told Woody.

"You are a *toy*!" exclaimed Woody. He had to get to Pizza Planet and find Andy! But Buzz wouldn't listen.

Woody finally convinced Buzz to hitch a ride with him on a Pizza Planet truck. When they got to the restaurant, Buzz immediately spotted a crane game that looked like a spaceship, and he climbed inside. He thought the ship would take him back to Star Command. Woody tried to pull Buzz out of the crane game. Unfortunately, Andy's mean neighbor, Sid, won both toys as prizes!

Sid took Buzz and Woody home to his scary bedroom. It was filled with mutant toys that Sid had made by taking his toys apart and putting them back together in horrible ways.

Terrified, Buzz and Woody tried to find a way to escape.

As they searched for a way out of Sid's house, Buzz spotted a TV playing a commercial for Buzz Lightyear toys. He was shocked to discover that Woody was right—he was just a toy after all.

Heartbroken, Buzz gave up on trying to escape.

A FLYING TOY
SPACE RANGER
LIGHTYEAR

Suddenly, Sid ran into the room and strapped a rocket to Buzz. Sid was planning to blow Buzz up the next day!

Woody knew they had to get away. But first, he had to convince Buzz that escaping was worthwhile.

"Over in that house is a kid who thinks you are the greatest, and it's not because you're a space ranger. It's because you're his toy!" explained Woody.

Finally, Buzz understood: being a toy *was* important. He had to get back to Andy!

Woody came up with a plan and asked Sid's mutant toys for help. As Sid was about to light Buzz's rocket, Woody and the mutants came to life and surrounded the mean boy.

"From now on, you must take good care of your toys. Because if you don't, we'll find out, Sid," said Woody. Sid ran away in terror—and the toys cheered!

Just then—*Honk! Honk!* Andy's family's moving van was leaving. They were moving to a new home . . . without Buzz and Woody!

Buzz and Woody ran as fast as they could to catch up with Andy's moving van. Andy's other toys tried to help them, but it was no use.

Suddenly, Buzz remembered the rocket on his back. Woody lit the fuse. *Whoosh!* He and Buzz shot upward. Just before the rocket exploded, Buzz opened his wings. The rocket snapped off, and Buzz and Woody went soaring through the air.

"Hey, Buzz!" cried Woody. "You're flying!"

Woody held on tight as Buzz aimed straight for Andy's car.

Buzz and Woody glided through the car's sunroof and landed on the backseat—right next to Andy.

"Woody! Buzz!" Andy exclaimed.

Both toys were glad to be back—right where they belonged.

Disney · PIXAR
TOY STORY 2

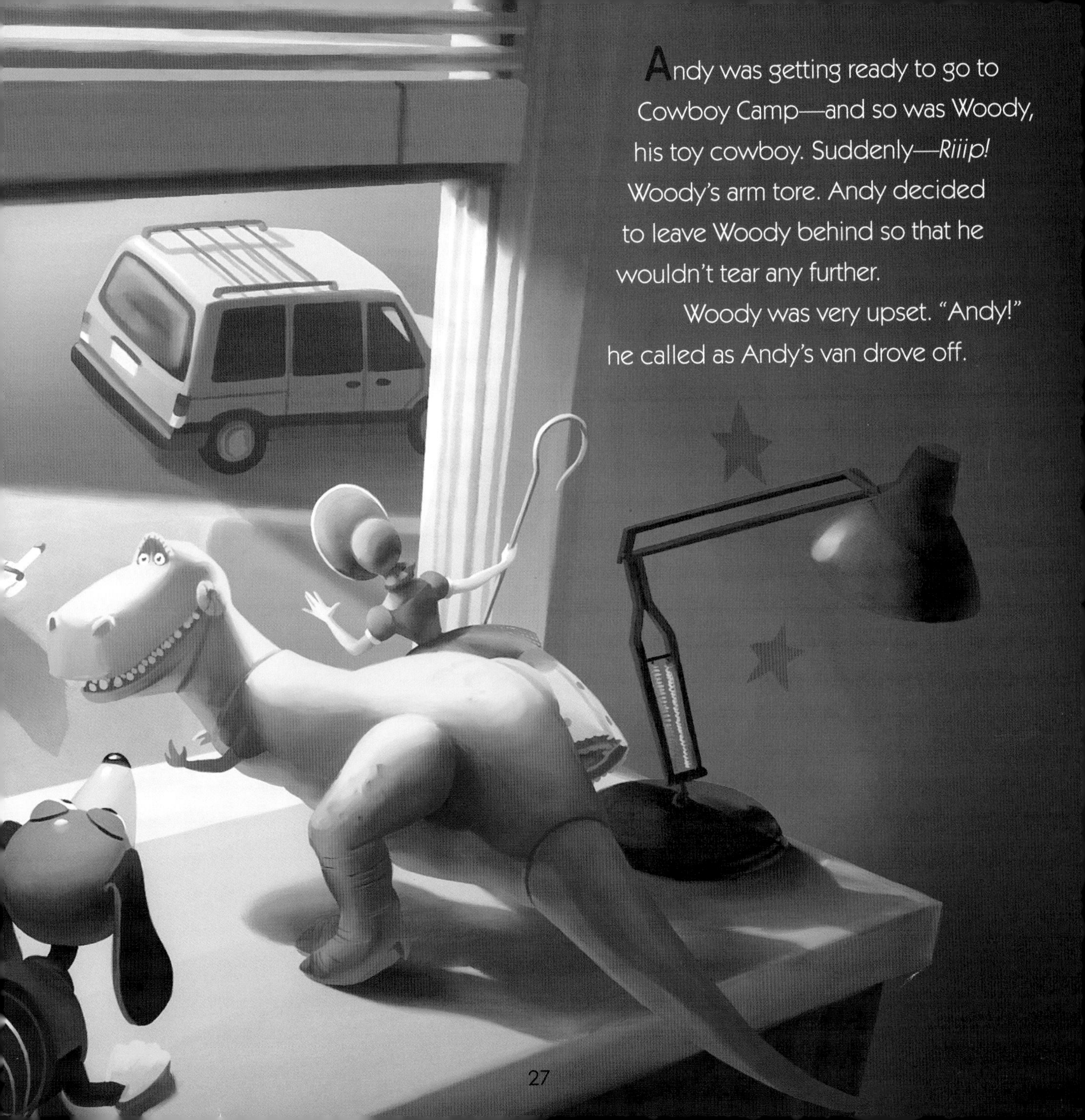

Andy was getting ready to go to Cowboy Camp—and so was Woody, his toy cowboy. Suddenly—*Riiip!* Woody's arm tore. Andy decided to leave Woody behind so that he wouldn't tear any further.

Woody was very upset. "Andy!" he called as Andy's van drove off.

While Andy was away, his mom held a yard sale. A strange man tried to buy Woody, who had been included in the sale by mistake.

"Sorry," Andy's mom told the man. "He's not for sale."

But the man wanted Woody . . . so he stole him!

Buzz Lightyear tried to catch up to the man's car as it sped away with Woody inside. But Buzz wasn't fast enough. All he saw was the license plate LZTYBRN and a few feathers floating out of the car's trunk.

Buzz and the rest of Andy's toys were determined to get Woody back. Using the clues Buzz had found, they figured out that the man who had stolen Woody was Al McWhiggin, the chicken-suit-wearing owner of Al's Toy Barn.

Buzz decided he had to go to Al's Toy Barn. "Who's with me?" he asked. The toys quickly put together a rescue party and set out in search of Woody.

Meanwhile, Al took Woody to his apartment. There Woody met the Roundup gang—Jessie the cowgirl, Bullseye the horse, and the Prospector. They had all been on an old TV show together—and Woody had been the star!

Woody couldn't believe it!

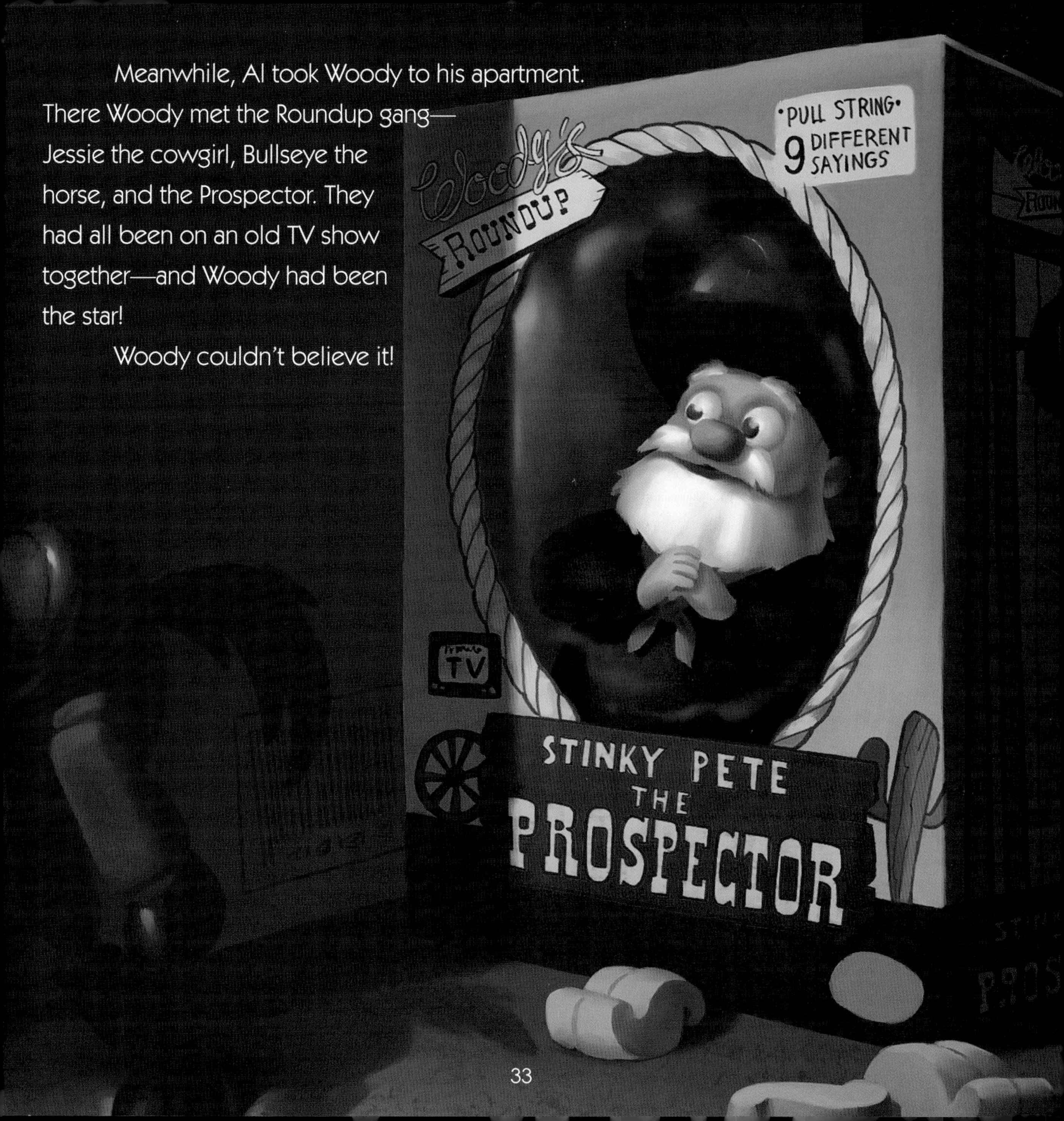

Jessie and Bullseye showed Woody a room full of Roundup gang collectibles, from posters to toys to an old record player. Woody had fun getting to know his new friends.

"Now it's on to the museum!" declared the Prospector. He explained that Al planned to sell the Roundup gang as a complete set to a toy museum in Japan.

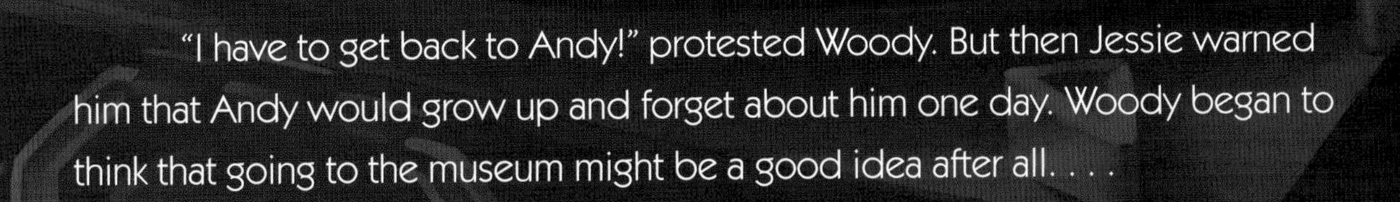

"I have to get back to Andy!" protested Woody. But then Jessie warned him that Andy would grow up and forget about him one day. Woody began to think that going to the museum might be a good idea after all. . . .

Suddenly, Buzz and his rescue party arrived. Woody explained that Jessie and Bullseye were his friends—and he didn't want to leave them.

"You're a toy!" Buzz said. "Life's only worth living if you're being loved by a kid." But Woody was still worried that Andy might not want him anymore. He decided to stay with the Roundup gang.

Disappointed, Buzz and the other toys left without Woody.

But as Woody watched *Woody's Roundup* on the TV, he began to miss Andy. Thinking it over, he realized that Buzz was right. He belonged with Andy.

Woody had an idea.

"Come with me!" he said to the Roundup gang. "Andy will play with all of us, I know it."

Woody, Jessie, and Bullseye prepared to leave—but the Prospector blocked their path! He was determined to go to the toy museum. He had never had an owner, and he didn't care about children. He wanted to stay in mint condition forever!

"Buzz! Guys! Help!" Woody called to his old friends.

Buzz and the toys turned back for their friend. Suddenly, Al arrived and packed Woody and the Roundup gang into a suitcase. He was taking them to the airport!

Buzz and Slinky tried to get Woody out of the suitcase, but the Prospector pulled him back in.

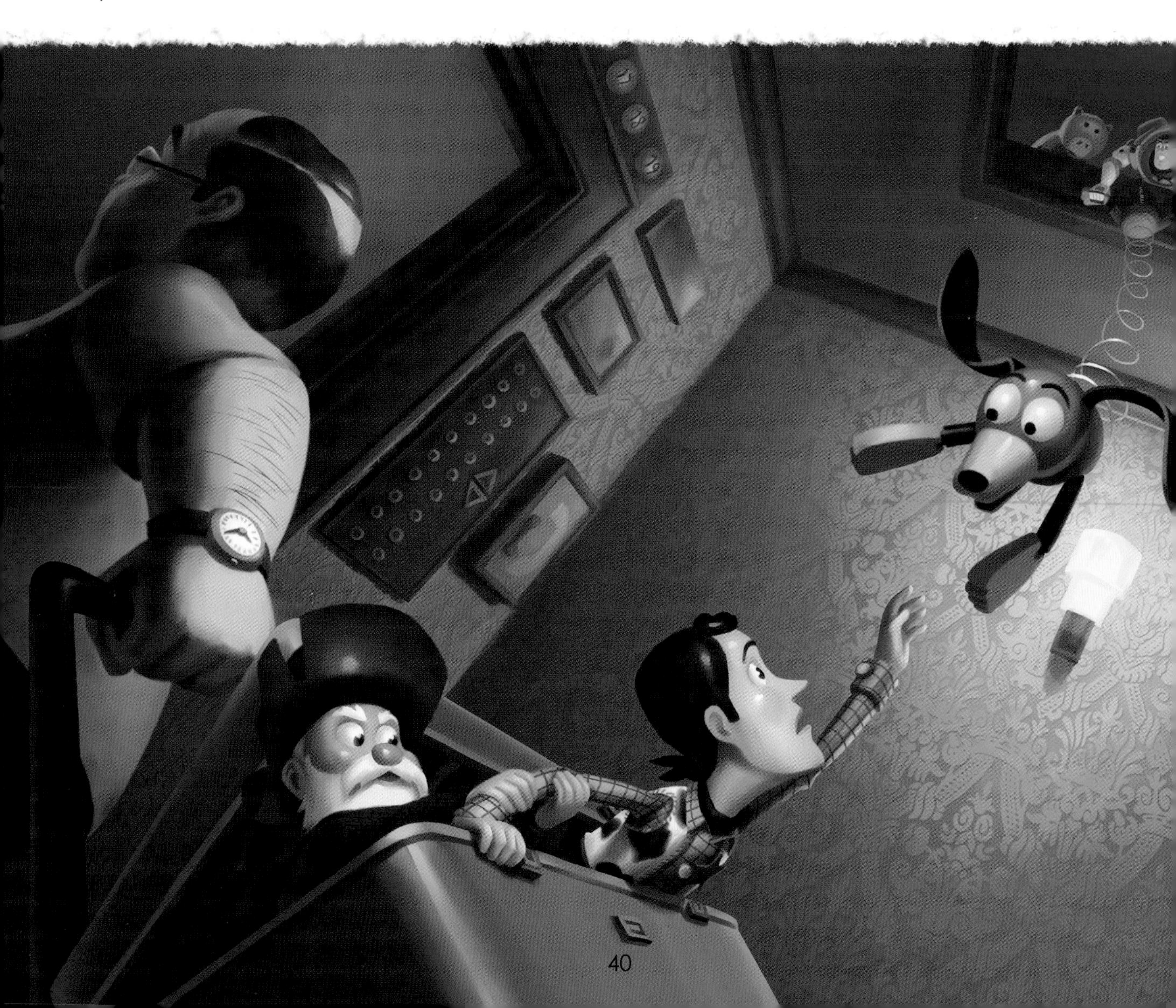

Woody's friends wouldn't give up. They found an empty truck outside Al's apartment and worked together to drive it to the airport.

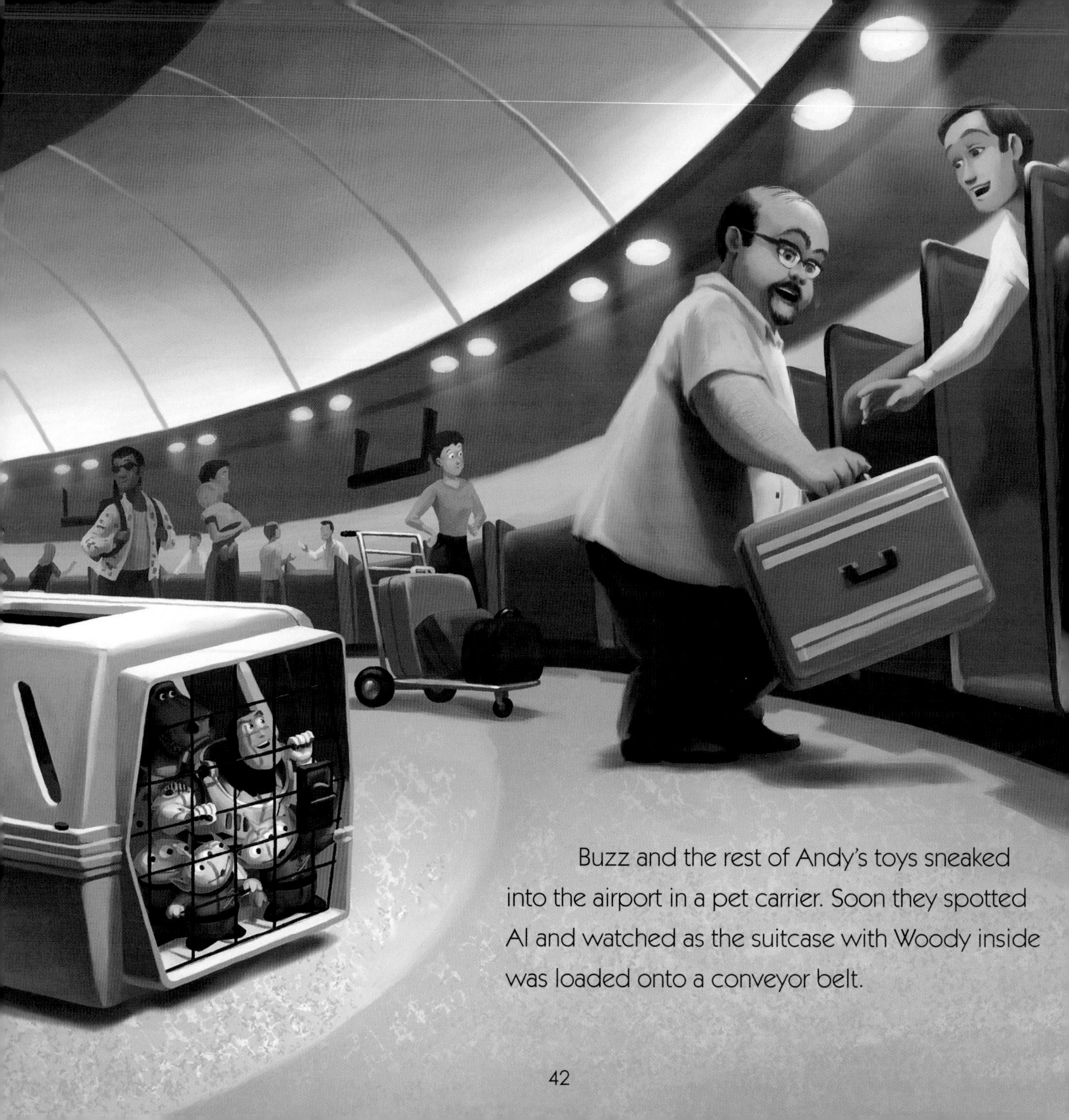

Buzz and the rest of Andy's toys sneaked into the airport in a pet carrier. Soon they spotted Al and watched as the suitcase with Woody inside was loaded onto a conveyor belt.

Buzz and Andy's other toys followed the suitcase. But when Buzz opened it, the Prospector wouldn't let Woody go without a fight. Together, Buzz and Woody trapped the Prospector in a nearby backpack and sent him off for good.

Bullseye hopped out of the suitcase just in time—but Jessie was trapped inside! Woody watched in horror as the suitcase was loaded onto a plane.

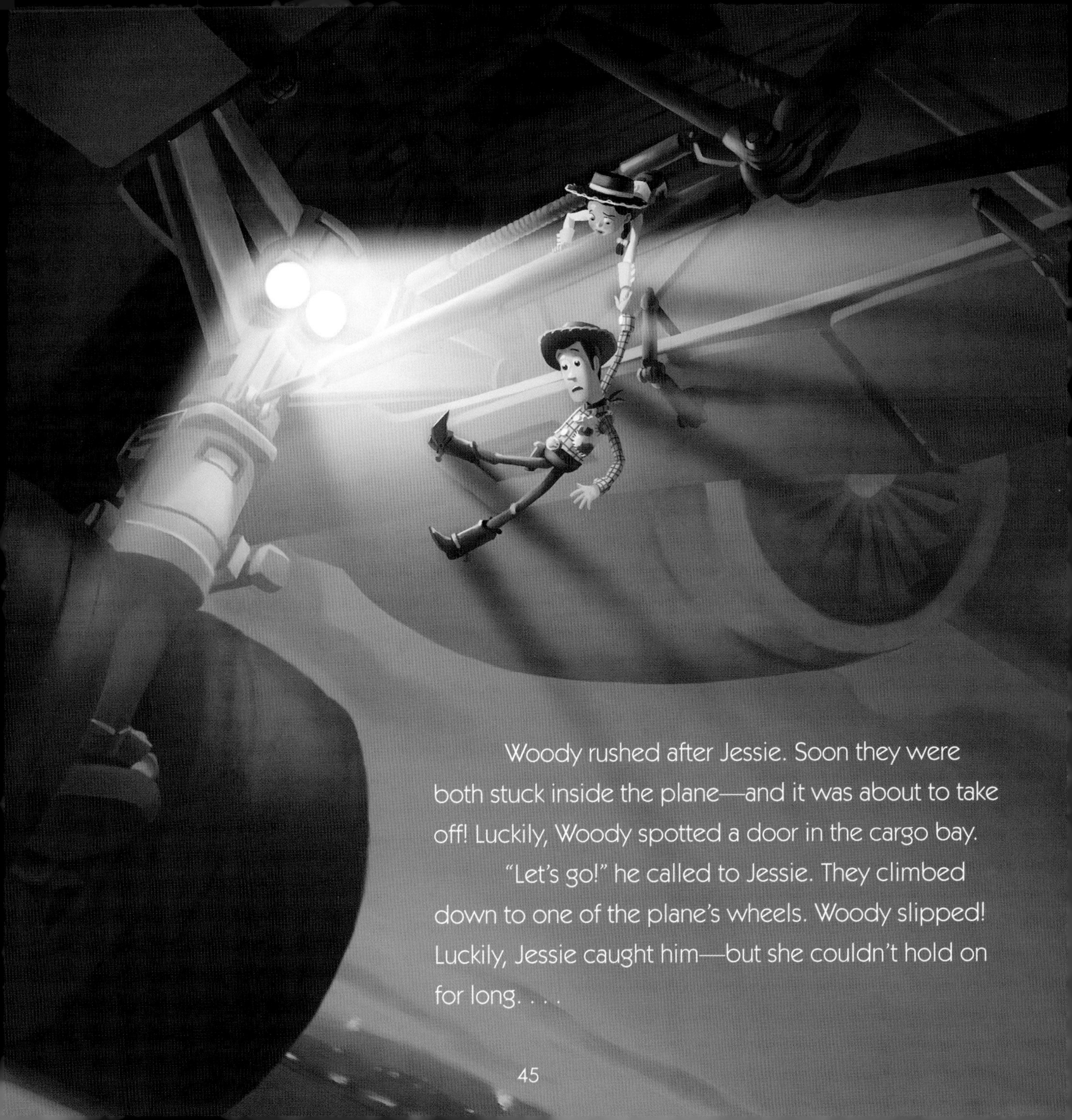

Woody rushed after Jessie. Soon they were both stuck inside the plane—and it was about to take off! Luckily, Woody spotted a door in the cargo bay.

"Let's go!" he called to Jessie. They climbed down to one of the plane's wheels. Woody slipped! Luckily, Jessie caught him—but she couldn't hold on for long. . . .

Dangling from the plane, Woody bravely used his pull string like a lasso. He took Jessie's hand, and together they swung down to the runway. Buzz and Bullseye were waiting to catch them.

"We did it!" cried Jessie. Everyone was safe!

"Let's go home," said Woody.

"Oh, wow!" Andy exclaimed when he got home from Cowboy Camp and found Jessie and Bullseye with all his favorite toys. "New toys!"

Andy and his toys—new and old—couldn't wait to have more adventures together.

Disney · PIXAR
TOY STORY 3

Andy was all grown up and getting ready to go off to college. Buzz, Woody, and the rest of his toys were worried. What would happen to them?

Woody wanted to stay at Andy's house. He loved Andy and was sure the toys would be stored safely in the attic.

But Jessie felt anxious. She still wanted to be played with!

"What's important is that we stay together," said Buzz.

When Jessie spotted a box of old toys in Andy's mom's car, she knew just what to do. The box was being donated to Sunnyside, the local daycare center. There'd be plenty of kids to play with there!

Woody followed the other toys into the box. He tried to convince them to stay, but the others were afraid Andy would throw them in the trash. Suddenly, Andy's mom got into the car and drove away. The toys were going to Sunnyside!

When Andy's toys arrived at the daycare center, a strawberry-scented bear named Lotso welcomed them with hugs. Lotso took them to the Caterpillar Room, where they would be staying.

Sunnyside seemed perfect. The toys couldn't wait to play with all the kids! Jessie was sure that going there had been the right choice.

Woody didn't feel the same way. He told his friends he was going back to Andy, with or without them.

The toys wanted to stay. So Woody left . . . alone.

The toys were sad to see Woody go. But soon after he walked out the door, the classroom bell rang. Playtime was about to start!

Unfortunately, playtime at Sunnyside wasn't what the toys had expected. The Caterpillar Room was for toddlers, who played roughly with their toys.

The toys were horrified as the little kids pulled, kicked, smashed, and bit them. They did *not* like playtime at Sunnyside.

Meanwhile, Woody had gotten stuck in a tree as he left Sunnyside.
A little girl named Bonnie found him and decided to take him home with her.

Bonnie introduced Woody to her toys at home, then played with all of them for hours. Woody hadn't had that much fun in a long time! But he was still determined to get back to Andy.

Back at Sunnyside, Buzz told Lotso that he and his friends wanted to leave the Caterpillar Room.

At first Lotso was friendly. But he soon turned nasty. He wouldn't let Buzz and his friends change to a different room. And he wouldn't let them leave Sunnyside at all!

With the help of a doll named Big Baby and the rest of his gang, Lotso flipped Buzz's reset switch. Buzz believed that he was a real space ranger—and that he worked for Lotso. The evil bear made Buzz lock up Jessie and the rest of Andy's toys.

The toys thought they were doomed—until Woody returned! He had realized that he shouldn't have left his friends. "From now on, we stick together," said Woody.

The toys had to get Buzz back—and get out of Sunnyside!

Working together, the toys came up with a plan.

First, they captured Buzz and reset him so that he was their friend again.

Next, they sneaked past Lotso's security. All they had to do was make it through the trash chute—and they'd be free!

But when the toys slid down the trash chute, Lotso and his gang were waiting for them!

"Why don't you come back and join our family again?" asked the mean bear with a sneer.

"This isn't a family, it's a prison!" cried Jessie.

Lotso ordered Big Baby to push Andy's toys into the Dumpster. But Big Baby didn't listen. He realized that Jessie was right and threw Lotso in the Dumpster instead!

Suddenly, a garbage truck arrived. When it picked up the Dumpster, Andy's toys tumbled into the truck with Lotso. They were going to the city dump!

At the dump, the toys were dropped onto a giant conveyor belt . . . headed right for a scary incinerator!

Lotso managed to escape. But when the others asked him for help, the mean bear ran away instead.

Luckily, the toy Aliens arrived just in time. They had found a claw and used it to save their friends!

Meanwhile, Lotso wasn't so lucky. A pair of garbagemen gave him a new home—and he did not like it one bit!

Woody, Buzz, and the others sneaked onto another garbage truck and rode all the way back to Andy's house. They climbed into a box marked ATTIC and watched as Andy prepared to leave for college.

Then Woody had an idea. . . .

As Andy packed his car, Woody stuck a note on the box full of toys. Andy read the address on the note and drove the box there—he was giving his toys to Bonnie!

"These are mine," Andy said to the little girl as he pulled his toys out of the box one by one. "But I'm going away now, so I need someone really special to look after them."

Andy knew he had found a loving home for his toys.

The toys watched as Andy pulled away.

"So long, partner," said Woody.

While they would always remember their time with Andy, the toys were excited about having new adventures with Bonnie.